Snap

Murmur

Slurp

Scrub

Mwahffff

Swoosh

Tap Tap

Chomp

Whirrr

Gurgle

Beep

Scrunch

Chitter Chatter

Flush

Clatter

Splosh

Splish Splash

Bang

Purrr

Clank

Pitter Patter

Woosh

Brmmmm

Ratatat  Hee Hee Hee

First published in 2017 by Child's Play (International) Ltd
Ashworth Road, Bridgemead, Swindon SN5 7YD, UK

Published in USA by Child's Play Inc
250 Minot Avenue, Auburn, Maine 04210

Distributed in Australia by Child's Play Australia Pty Ltd
Unit 10/20 Narabang Way, Belrose, Sydney, NSW 2085

ISBN 978-1-84643-887-5
CLP260916CPL11168875

Printed in Shenzhen, China

1 3 5 7 9 10 8 6 4 2

A catalogue record of this book
is available from the British Library

www.childs-play.com

Quiet!

Kate Alizadeh

Creeeeaak

Sssh! Listen,
what's that noise?

It's the bubbling of the pan
and the humming of the fridge.

It's me tapping on the table
and my brother banging his spoon.

It's the cat chewing her food and my dad laughing away.

Burble

Ping

Clank

wish

Tiptoe

Meow

Sssh! Listen, what's that noise?

It's the TV babbling, as I zoom zoom the car across the rug and the cat purrs.

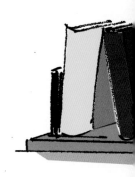

Blah Blah Blah

Flicker

Chatter

Babble

Purrrr

Brrmm

Zooom

And the dog snoring and the laptop whirring
and the pitter patter of the rain against the window.

It's my brother rattling his toys
and giggling when I tickle his feet.

Rustle

Swish

Meow

Tingaling

Jingle Jangle

And the swish and rustle as I turn the pages of my book.

Sssh! Listen,

what's that noise?

It's the water dripping from the taps and the splish splash of my bath. And the squeak squeak of my rubber duck and the swoosh of the flush.

It's the whirring of the hairdryer.

And the scrubbing of my toothbrush
and the gurgle of the water down the sink.

Tick Tock

Twang   Bang

Click

Creeeaak

Ssssh! Listen,
what's that noise?

Click

It's the creak of the floorboards
and the bed squeaking.

It's the soft hushed voice of my dad
as he reads me a bedtime story.
And his deep quiet voice as he sings a lullaby.

And the flip flop of his friendly feet...

as he clicks off the switch.

And blows me a goodnight kiss.

Ssshh! Listen, it's so quiet.

Fizzle

Sizzle

Bang   Swish

Jingle Jangle

Pitter Patter

Fizz

Squeak

Creaak

La lala

Hummmm

Click

Zzzzzz

Ding

Eeeeek

Ping

Hahaha

Plish Plish

Ring

Drip Drip

Buzz

Flip Flop

Rattle